MW00873350

Grandma Bunny

The Forest Herbalist

Written by Jenifer Bliss
Illustrations by D.R. Griffis

Grandma Bunny,
The Forest Herbalist

Original Text Self-Copyright © 1993 by
Jenifer Pederson-Bliss
aka Coyote Jen
Copyright © 2016 by Jenifer Victoria Bliss
Artwork Copyright © 2016 by David Randolph Griffis
All rights reserved. No part of this publication may be
reproduced, stored in a retrieval system, or transmitted in any
form or by any means, electronic, mechanical, photocopying,
recording, or otherwise, without written permission of the
publisher:
Sierra Muses Press

An affiliate of Sea Turtle Press
P.O. Box 942, N. San Juan, California 95960
mountainbliss8@gmail.com
drgshadycreek@gmail.com

ISBN 13: 978-0-9912102-4-4
ISBN 10: 0-9912102-4-7

Printed in the USA

*May the healing power of Nature guide you into
a future of health, wisdom, purpose, and
moments of great happiness.*

Table of Contents

Grandma Bunny's Recipes

Grandma Bunny comes in from the rain.

1

Grandma Bunny

In a mossy green forest, amid tall pines, fir and cedars, below a canopy of large shield ferns, is a warren, a hole in the ground where the bunny family lives. There, nestled under the gnarled roots of a very old fir tree, is our underground home. I live there with Papa Bunny, Mama Bunny and my three little bunny brothers.

Grandma Bunny, who this story is about, didn't live with us at first, she just came to visit from time to time. Anyway, she was a very special rabbit. Of course, everyone thinks their grandmother is special, but Grandma Bunny was important to many other creatures in the forest besides us. One of my earliest memories of her was during a huge storm. The rain had been coming down for days. There was flooding in the valley, and we were all very worried, as rabbits often are.

A flash of lightning set us all trembling, and we hopped to Mama, clinging to her and to each other as thunder crashed down upon us.

"It is all right children," Mama Bunny reassured us. "We are safe here in our warm burrow." But Julian, James, Jerome and I clung to her with our digging claws and shivered.

There was another flash and deafening boom. Jerome began to cry, "We're all going to be killed." And that started us crying and shivering even more.

"Oh phooey," said Papa. "I know it's scary, but I've been in hundreds of storms like this one. None of us will be killed."

Suddenly, there was a knock at the door.

"Who would be out in this weather?" Papa wondered out loud. We all stood perfectly still and watched as Papa slowly opened the door and raised his paws, ready to box. Rabbits are good boxers and do this to protect their young. But Papa lowered his paws, "It is Grandma Bunny! Penelope, What a surprise."

"Hello," said Grandma Bunny with a big, toothy smile. She was sopping wet.

Papa took her bags and lifted the poncho off her head.

"Thank you, Jack," Grandma said.

Mama hopped over and gave her mother a big, nose-to-nose kiss. We, little bunnies were still hiding.

"Hello my kittens," Grandma grinned as we peeked out from our hiding places.

Julian pointed from beneath the table, "Your boots are all muddy."

"Oh, you're right," said Grandma, and she sat down to unlace them. "You know, this is my favorite weather."

"You like this?" James asked as he crawled out from under the chest.

"It is magic," Grandma said with sparkles in her eyes. "The flashes of lightening, the sudden hard rain and the KA-BOOM of thunder -- so powerful like it is exploding inside your whole body. I do like it!"

"But aren't you afraid?" I asked, stepping out from behind the curtain.

"Not anymore. But, when I was a little kit, I remember hopping from window to window, crying and yelling that we would all be killed."

"That is what Jerome did a little while ago," I said, and pointed at the huge bulge in the back of Mama's skirt. Jerome peeked out, and we all started laughing.

Julian sniffed Grandma's bags. "What's in here?"

"Oh, lots of interesting things," Grandma smiled, but just at that moment, there was another flash of lightning and an ear-splitting KA-BOOM. We froze and all looked at Grandma Bunny who stared back at us with wild delight.

"Are you a witch?" James asked her.

"Oh, dear heavens," Grandma laughed, "though I can understand why someone might think so. I am a bit odd compared to most civilized animals. No, I am not a witch, but I do believe in magic. You can't get away from it. Magic is all around. The Earth and the trees are magic. Your thoughts are magic. Why, your very existence is magic. When you are old and sophisticated, it is sometimes easy to forget about the magic of life. But all you have to do is go for a long hop in the forest, and you can feel it, pulsing through everything -- the wind, the trees, all the plants, the streams, the soil and each animal. Magic is everywhere."

Julian crawled out from under the table, "I think that you *are* magic, Grandma Bunny."

Grandma Bunny got another glimmer in her eye. "I think I am too, but no more than you or anyone else."

"Ouch," came a whimper from the corner.

"It's Jerome," Mama said. He had hopped back to bed and was hiding under his blanket. "He's got a terrible earache," she said, "and you know how terrible earaches can be, especially for rabbits."

Grandma Bunny hopped to Jerome and lifted a long, droopy ear that flopped to one side. "I'm sorry dear," she said knowingly. She rummaged in one of her bags. "Just last night I made some fresh garlic and mullein flower oil. Now we'll just warm this up on the wood stove and put a dropper full in your ear."

Grandma Bunny helping Jerome feel better.

"You just lay here on your side," she told Jerome. Then she put the warm oil in his ear.

Jerome closed his eyes as the warm oil soothed the pain in his ear.

After a half hour, Grandma hopped over and put a napkin in Jerome's ear, and when he sat up, the extra oil ran out into the napkin. Grandma rubbed the top of his head with her nose, "You should feel much better tomorrow."

Our meadow,
where the oak and the pine meet.

We all gaze at the vast, nighttime sky.

2

Herbal Gifts

While the clouds dumped more rain outside, Papa, Julian, James, Grandma and I dug trenches to keep the water from running into our warren. When we were done, we all sat around the fire to eat long grasses and root soup.

Grandma Bunny patted her tummy and said, "Good meal Mama Bunny!" Then she took a fancy bottle out of her bag. It looked like a treasure she had found in the recycling bin. "This is for Papa Jack."

Papa looked at the dark, blue bottle.

"It is an herbal cordial for your heart," said Grandma. "It has hawthorn berries and flowers, motherwort leaves, borage flowers, wild oats, lemon balm and honey from Amigo Bob's bees."

"Amigo Bob's bees?" Papa took a little nip and smiled. "It tastes delicious!"

Next Grandma Bunny took out a little bag with purple violets embroidered on the front. "This is for Jerome," she said, smiling at him. "There are violet leaves and flowers, to help break up that congestion you get with those nagging colds. I also brought you a big bottle of purple cone flower and astragalus root tincture with homemade apple cider vinegar and honey to help you stay healthy!"

Jerome hopped over and sniffed the violets. He was kind of shy, so he blinked his big eyes at Grandma Bunny, his way of saying thank you, and Grandma Bunny said, "You are welcome."

"Let's see…for Mama…" Grandma pulled out a bunch of roots tied together with a string made from nettles. "These are

7

black cohosh roots, from Ba's herb garden - to help ease those cramps and headaches you've been complaining about with your cycles."

Mama took a bite of the dried root and put the bundle of roots against her heart. "Thank you, Grandma Bunny."

Grandma Bunny smiled, then turned a scrunched eye toward the boy kittens. With a pirate accent she said, "For Julian, James and Jerome, I brought... poison antidote." She pulled out 3 little glass vials – more bottles she likely got from the recycling bin outside Robyn Martin's homeopathic herb room. They were tied with cords made from nettle and blackberry fibers and long enough so that the boys could wear them around their necks. "I hear you boys like to capture little snakes and spiders and other such lovely creatures. So, you should never be without your poison antidotes. It helps to take the sting and pain out of a bite." Grandma lifted her eyebrows in a mischievous sort of way and continued in her pirate voice, "It's got ledum, purple cone flower roots, black cohosh roots and calendula in it." The boys put the cords over their heads and hopped around the burrow growling, "We are invincible! Ha, ha, ha, ha."

Mama stood up, "Well, I suppose I should start the cookies now."

"I'll help," Grandma offered, and they got up and went into the kitchen.

All of a sudden, I began to feel very sad. Grandma Bunny had brought something for everyone except me. Tears rolled down my face. I tried to hold them in, but I couldn't. I was forgotten.

Mama saw me, "What is wrong, Jenny?"

Big tears clogged my nose and my nostrils kept twitching as I sobbed. "I didn't get a gift, Mama."

Grandma Bunny hopped over, "Oh, that is not true. I just left yours outside and forgot for a minute." She took my paw and led me outside the warren door. There, getting just enough rain to keep them happy were eight little plants in a willow basket.

"This is a very special gift for you, Jenny. These plants are alive. If you take good care of them, they will grow big and give you lots of medicine. They will be your friends." She pointed her paw, "This one is Oregon grape, this one - black cohosh, yarrow, calendula, comfrey, garlic, nasturtium and this one is lavender.

I sniffed the plants.

"I hope," Grandma Bunny said, "that this will be the beginning of a life-long love of herbs and healing." She smiled, showing her big, front teeth. "Together, we will make medicine from them. And, I will teach you what I know."

I wiped my wet eyes with the back of my paw and sniffled a smile. I knew that plants were very important to Grandma Bunny, but more than that, she had promised to spend her time with me. "Thank you," I sniffled as she wrapped her paws around me in one of her warm, furry hugs.

Grandma Bunny digs in her basket for Aloe Vera and
other herbs to treat Old Mister Beaver's foot.

3

Mister Beaver

Grandma looked out the warren door, "The storm is broken. The clouds are moving on. This is a great time to go for a hop!"

"But it is all wet outside," Julian said.

Grandma's eyes were big with excitement, "Yes, but it is beautiful, wild and magic."

We didn't have to be asked twice. Papa, Julian, James and I fluffed up our fur and jumped right out into the crisp night air. Mama stayed home with Jerome because of his ear. "Be careful for owls and foxes," she warned.

We hopped through the brush to the top of Buttercup Hill, keeping our ears perked up for danger, as Mama told us to do. At the top of the hill the whole sky opened up, and we could see from horizon to horizon. I took a deep breath. Above us the stars sparkled more brightly than I ever remembered.

"Look bunnies," Grandma Bunny pointed to a group of stars that looked like a dipper. "That is Ursa Major. Ursa means *bear*, and major means *big*. So Ursa Major is the big bear. If you follow those two stars on the side of the dipper, as if they were an arrow, you will see the North Star, and the North Star is the tail of the little bear, Ursa Minor. Minor means little." Then she showed us Orion the Hunter, Canis Major, Orion's dog and the big star, Sirius in the dog's collar.

James snuggled close. "Stars are awesome," he whispered. They are so bright. There are so many of them."

I wiped his snout with the back of my paw.

Grandma hummed, "Each star is a sun like our own sun, but those stars are so far away that they look small."

"Looking at them makes me feel tiny," I purred. "At least compared to the vastness of the universe."

Papa hummed, and we all hummed together.

*****

As we hopped home through the brush, we heard a noise. We stopped and stood perfectly still, turning our ears to listen. We looked in every direction, without moving our heads, and sniffed, the way all rabbits do, to make sure that we were not in any danger from owls, foxes, coyotes or bobcats, which we fear most. But it wasn't any of those things. Someone was whispering loudly. "Penelope. Penelope. Is that you?"

"It is all right bunnies," Grandma reassured us. "It's Mr. Beaver. He is a friend. Yes, Mr. Beaver, it is me, Penelope." Grandma Bunny hopped toward the voice. We followed her with our paws up, ready to box or scratch should there be any trouble, but soon we could see Mr. Beaver's figure silhouetted against the stars. Panting and out of breath, Mr. Beaver sighed, "Penelope, I've been looking for you for hours."

"What seems to be the problem?" Grandma asked.

"It's my dad. He cut his foot on a piece of broken glass while gnawing down a tree, and it is all swollen and infected. Doctor Mouse says he is very concerned about it. But my father said, 'Go get Penelope Rabbit. She'll know what to do.' So, well, here I am."

Grandma turned her big eyes on us. "I have to go, but I need to get my medicine basket first." Grandma started hopping home, but then she turned and caught my eye. "You can come with me, Jenny, if you want." I guess she picked me because I was the oldest and most interested in her work. In any case, we got her medicine basket, fluffed up our fur and followed Mr. Beaver into the night.

The Beavers' house was very difficult to get to because it was in the middle of the pond, plus it was dark. Also, the front door was underwater. Rabbits don't like to swim, so Mr. Beaver made a small door on the side of his home -- just for us. We stepped onto a log, and he floated Grandma and me out to the den. Once inside, the den was cozy and warm. Mrs. Beaver smiled, "would you like some waterlily tea?"

"Yes, please," Grandma Bunny said, "but first let me see what's going on with Old Ben.

"Hi there, Ben," she said, stepping over the pile of sticks that he had been chewing.

Old Mr. Beaver spit some splinters and slapped the floor with his tail. "Penelope. I'm so glad to see you. Dr. Mouse told me that if my foot isn't visibly better by tomorrow, that serious intervention will have to be taken. But, I told him I'd go see you, and that I wouldn't be needing his help."

Grandma peeled off Old Mr. Beaver's sock, exposing his foot. The skin under his fur was swollen with oozing pus. Grandma twitched her nose as she always did when she was assessing a situation.

"This is a doozy Ben. I'll do what I can, but if it doesn't work, you will have to go back to Dr. Mouse."

Old Mr. Beaver got a sad look on his face. He sat back on his log and closed his eyes. There was a long silence. Grandma Bunny closed her eyes too. I watched her face.

Suddenly a big smile crossed Old Mr. Beaver's lips. He looked up at Grandma Bunny. "Penelope," he slapped the floor with his tail, "I know you can help me."

"OK Ben," she smiled, "I'll do my best."

In the kitchen with Mrs. Beaver, Grandma Bunny made a strong tea of Oregon grape root, rosemary and thyme.

"It tastes bitter," she said, handing Mr. Beaver a cup. "But it will heal you from the inside and work as a cleansing wash that you can use morning and evening. However, if anything can heal your foot, it will be fresh aloe vera." She looked up at Mrs. Beaver because she knew that Mrs. Beaver would be taking care of Old Mr. Beaver's foot. "Wash the wound with the tea, then bandage it up with a nice slab of fresh aloe leaf -- slimy part right over the wound. And when the sun is out, let the wound get some fresh air and sunlight."

Grandma Bunny pulled three large, succulent aloe vera leaves from her medicine basket. They seemed more like swords to me, with their sharp spines. "These are from Deborah's Greenhouse," I chimed in. "She cultivates the most beautiful aloe plants."

Mrs. Beaver took the leaves and covered them in pine bark to keep them fresh.

Grandma smiled, "Deborah, would be happy to know that you are using her medicine."

Old Mr. Beaver took a sip of his tea and made a terrible grimace. "Uck, yuck, this is awful!"

Grandma Bunny laughed. "I told you it would be."

Old Mr. Beaver gave her a cocky smile but drank it up.

Grandma washed the dirt and debris from Old Mr. Beaver's foot, then cleaned it carefully with the herbal tea. Next, she sliced open the fresh aloe leaf (cutting off the spines) and put the aloe slab, slime side, right over the wound. Finally, Grandma Bunny wrapped Old Mr. Beaver's whole foot in 3 large mullein leaves and tied them in place with a long cattail. "Do this two-times a day," she said, "giving it time to breathe between, and don't forget to have a cup of tea at the same time. I know it is your favorite," she laughed.

"Speaking of tea," Mrs. Beaver lifted up a steaming mug. "I've got some waterlilies brewing and sunflower seed cookies."

I looked at Grandma and smiled.

"Of course," said Grandma. We pulled up sitting logs near Old Mister Beaver. And while we sipped, Mrs. Beaver pointed to the mud drawings on the walls. "These are the new dams my grandchildren have built." She brushed a spiderweb from the wall. "I am so proud of my grandchildren, except Little Ben Junior. I had such hopes for him. Then he ran off with Miss Porcupine … a mixed marriage, you know. He didn't even build a dam for them to live in. Miss Porcupine wanted a burrow. So Little Ben Jr. dug a spacious burrow for her. Of all things," said Mrs. Beaver, "a beaver digging burrows."

I could tell that she spent a great deal of time thinking about it. "You must love Little Ben Jr. very much," I whispered.

14

"What!" Mrs. Beaver slapped the wall with her tail and looked at me with a 'how dare you' sort of look.

"I, I only meant that it probably wouldn't bother you so much if you didn't care about him."

Mrs. Beaver frowned and looked at the floor. "I suppose. He was such a sweet little beaver and so good at gnawing down trees."

"I bet he loves you too," Grandma Bunny added.

"It always seemed so when he was young," Mrs. Beaver reminisced. "He was my favorite grandchild until that disappointment."

Grandma looked over at Old Mr. Beaver, who had fallen asleep. "How are you feeling Ben?"

He let out a loud snore and muttered, "We'll just chew down that tree over there."

He must have been dreaming.

"Wake up, Ben" Mrs. Beaver hollered.

Old Mister Beaver opened one lid and made eye contact with Grandma Bunny who twitched her nose. "Imagine your foot better than ever," she said, "and be prepared to see Dr. Mouse if it doesn't look good. He is very wise and has lots of experience."

Old Mr. Beaver smiled his big toothy grin, "It will get better," he said with determination. His teeth, I noticed, were even bigger than Grandma Bunny's. Their eyes met, and after a long moment Grandma Bunny said, "I believe you, Ben."

The younger Mr. Beaver took out his firefly lamp and grabbed a few sunflower cookies from the table. "I can take you bunnies home now, if you like?"

We fluffed up our fur to keep warm and said goodnight to the beaver family.

*****

At home in the warren, everyone was curled up together in the sleeping burrow. We brushed our teeth, then sleepily cuddled in with the rest of the big, mass of snoring fur, our family.

Mrs. Squirrel scampers down the Madrone Tree.

4

Raphael - The Baby Squirrel

The next morning, Grandma and I put on our heavy coats and gloves to pick nettles in Ba's Garden. As we were hopping down the path, Grandma looked over at me. A glimmer sparkled in her eye.

"What are you thinking Grandma?" I asked.

"Oh, I was just thinking about last night. I was very proud of what you said to Mrs. Beaver. It must have taken a lot of courage."

I smiled.

"Too often," Grandma continued, "animals get caught up in their disappointments of each other and forget how precious someone is to them. The little things get too big, and the big thing, how much they love one another, is forgotten. I'm proud of you because your heart seems to know what is important. If you learn nothing else, that alone will help you to be a great healer."

"Oh Grandma," I said, smiling so much that my nose wrinkled up, and I had to sniffle, "Thank you for saying that." She always knew how to make me feel good about myself.

*****

With our bags full of nettles, we started hopping home. We hadn't gone far when Mrs. Squirrel came scampering down from a nearby madrone tree.

"Penelope! Penelope! I need your help. It's Raphael, my little son. He's very sick. He's had heart trouble since he was born. We've given him hawthorne berries every day, but he seems to be worse."

Mr. Squirrel backed slowly down the tree with little Raphael held over his shoulder. When he got to the bottom of the tree, Grandma Bunny hopped over and looked carefully at Raphael. After a long moment, she said, "There are some things that Nature cannot cure. Let's not waste any time. Take him to Dr. Mouse!"

*****

Dr. Mouse took a stethoscope from around his neck and listened to Raphael's heart. Then he used a fancy machine called an echocardiogram to see inside the heart. "There is a large hole in Raphael's heart," Dr. Mouse announced. "If you want him to live, we must schedule him for surgery as soon as possible."

Mr. and Mrs. Squirrel looked at each other in horror. They didn't like doctors or surgeries, but they wanted their son to live. Needless to say, they scheduled Raphael's surgery for the next morning. "Don't worry," Grandma Bunny said, "Dr. Mouse has the best hands for doing surgical procedures, and he is very careful."

Dr. Mouse kept Raphael in the hospital that night and hooked him up to a big machine that made it easier for him to breathe.

Grandma and I went home and made an extra big dinner so we could take some good, homemade food to Mr. and Mrs. Squirrel. Grandma also made some relaxing catnip, chamomile and fennel tea to help soothe Mr. and Mrs. Squirrel's nerves and aid their digestion. Then she asked me, "Jenny, please get my basket of homeopathic remedies. They don't allow you to give patients herbs in the hospital, but homeopathic remedies are acceptable. They are vibrational remedies, but that doesn't stop them from working. We'll also take along some of Robyn Martin's Arnica and Rescue Remedy so that Mr. and Mrs. Squirrel can give some to Raphael -- and take some

18

themselves." Grandma looked at me with a worried look in her eye. So, we drank some chamomile, catnip and fennel tea too, because hospitals can be pretty stressful places.

*****

Mr. and Mrs. Squirrel were very happy to have the nut loaf and root soup that we made for them. Raphael couldn't eat before his surgery, so Mr. Squirrel and then Mrs. Squirrel took turns eating with us in the cafeteria. Mrs. Squirrel started to cry when she saw us. She was so concerned about Raphael and so busy taking care of him that she hadn't been able to cry. Grandma Bunny stroked her fur, and Mrs. Squirrel covered her face with her tail and cried more. "You need to get all those emotions out," Grandma Bunny said. "Then you can be strong for Raphael." After a while, Mrs. Squirrel sat up and wiped the tears from her eyes. She ate some nut loaf and drank some tea, then scampered back to the hospital room to be with Raphael.

We were all worried about Raphael. His condition was extremely serious, and even with surgery, he could still die. Grandma whispered to me that part of any herbalist's remedies was the ability to pray, so when Mr. Squirrel came back, we all held paws and asked the Great Spirit of the Forest and all of Raphael's squirrel angels to surround him with healing light, help him get through the surgery and be strong and healthy for the rest of his life.

5

Trouble in the Forest

Weeks later, Grandma Bunny asked me, "Jenny, will you go out to the Beaver dam and check on Old Mr. Beaver?"

"Of course," I said and grabbed my foraging basket to gather horsetail grass on my way home.

When I got to the dam, Mr. Beaver was swimming in the pond with his grandchildren.

"Howdy, Jenny," Old Mr. Beaver hollered. Then he rolled over on his back and waved with his tail.

One of his grandsons swam up to him, "Watch this Grandpa," and the little beaver slapped his tail on the water. The little beaver looked different from the others. He had quills on the top of his head, kind of like his mother, Elenore Porcupine, Little Ben Jr.'s wife.

"Will you teach me how to do that, Quills?" Old Mister Beaver asked.

"Of course, Grandpa," Quills answered, splashing us all with water.

Old Mister Beaver smiled at his grandson. He didn't mind that the little beaver was different from the others. He loved him just the same.

"This is how you do it Grampa," Quills slapped the water with his tail again.

Old Mr. Beaver flung his tail into the air and dropped it onto the surface of the water, pretending that he was just learning how to do it for the first time.

I smiled, "I've come to look at your foot Mr. Beaver."

Mr. Beaver swam over to the edge of the pond and stuck his foot out on the bank. There was only a scar, but other than that, it looked good. "How does it feel?" I asked.

"It feels as good as ever!" he said with a big grin. "And you can just tell your grandmother Penelope, that I am indebted to her. Yes Mam, miraculous." He slapped the water with his tail and splashed me. "In fact, you can tell anyone I said so."

I smiled and shook his paw, "I will Mr. Beaver. I will."

As I was hopping down the path, I started thinking about Raphael. I wondered how he was doing and decided to check in on him. Before I even got to his tree, an acorn hit the ground right in front of my feet. It would have hit me in the head if I hadn't slowed down. Then another acorn fell and another, and soon it was raining acorns.

"What is going on?" I shouted and lifted my paws to box. Then I heard someone chuckling in the branches and looked up to see Raphael.

"Why you little scamp," I said and shook my paws at him. "I was just hopping over to see how you were doing."

Raphael giggled. It had only been four weeks since we didn't know if he would live or die. "I'm glad you are feeling better," I said, and threw a paw-full of acorns back at him.

At home in the burrow, Grandma Bunny was sitting down with Old Mr. Porcupine, the acupuncturist, Elenore Porcupine's dad. They were discussing different types of herbal medicine. Mr. Porcupine was an herbalist too. I set down my basket of horsetail grasses and rubbed my nose against Grandma Bunny's cheek. They both smiled at me to acknowledge my presence and continued their conversation.

So, Penelope," Mr. Porcupine asked, "Of all the medicinal herbs in the forest and gardens, which ones do you feel are the most valuable?"

Grandma thought for a moment, then she said, "It's not any particular medicinal herb that keeps animals well. The basis for health lies in what we eat every day. That is the key to health. We certainly eat food much more than we take medicine. Everything we put into our bodies either builds them or breaks them down. Well, for example, the animals who eat the human's garbage are always sick. While the animals who eat the whole, natural foods of the forest are almost always well. Yes," Grandma continued, "our food is our best medicine. In fact, many good herbs are great foods."

"I agree," said Mr. Porcupine. "But let's say with injuries for example, what medicinal herbs do you put at the top of the list?"

Well," said Grandma Bunny, "There is no question, Comfrey is the herb for any injury where the skin or bone is broken. It is called the knitting herb for a good reason. It knits tissues back together in no time. And if there is an infection, nasturtiums, Oregon grape root, garlic and onions have no rival as mild, yet very effective antibiotics."

"Yes, I do agree with you on that as well," nodded Mr. Porcupine. "That is why this latest news is bothering me so much."

Grandma Bunny gave him a puzzled look.

"It is being rumored," Mr. Porcupine continued, "that the Fox Den Administration is going to make comfrey and nasturtiums illegal."

"Why?" Grandma Bunny asked, obviously disturbed.

Mr. Porcupine looked up with a sarcastic face. "I suppose it is because they are effective medicines, and that they don't want any competition for their patented drugs,"

"That is disturbing news," Grandma said, getting up and thumping the floor with her foot. "Whatever shall we do?"

"That is a good question," said Mr. Porcupine. "The Fox Den Administration is a very powerful organization. They've got the ability to do whatever they like because the pharmaceutical companies give them lots of power, food, money and whatever else they want."

Grandma shook her head and wrinkled her nose, "But we should try to prove to them that these herbs are safe and effective. Granted, not all of them should be used every day as food, but both of these herbs are fine medicines to be used as needed."

Mr. Porcupine raised his quills and said, "The Fox Den Administration makes the argument that most animals will use something all the time if they think it's good for them."

"Some will," said Grandma Bunny, "but they do the same thing with the patented medicines. This is crazy!"

Mr. Porcupine rubbed his chin with the back of his paw, "I hope that the Fox Den Administration will listen to us and not just bully us around."

The place where we gather horsetail grass.

6

The Fox Den Administration

Not long after Grandma Bunny and Mr. Porcupine had
their conversation, I had a bad dream:

"Grandma? Where are you, Grandma, Grandma Bunny?"
It was very, very dark. I could hardly see the path in front of
me. Somehow, I had lost Grandma Bunny. I was all alone.
"Grandma!" Something was wrong, and then I smelled the
unmistakable scent of fox. I tried to hop, but my big feet got
tangled in some vines. "Grandma!" I screamed.

"Jenny. Wake up, Jenny." It was Grandma Bunny's
reassuring voice. "I'm right there." She nuzzled her nose into
my ear. "You had a bad dream. Everything is OK now."

I grabbed her fur and rubbed my chin all over her face.
"There were foxes in my dream," I panted, "and I couldn't
find you."

Grandma stroked my fur and slipped a little pillow under
my head. "Everything is all right now," she whispered.

The pillow smelled like lavender and lemon balm. My
eyes felt heavy. Grandma was right here. Before I knew it, I
was asleep again, and my bad dream faded.

*****

However, the next day I was in the kitchen, helping
Mama prepare beet burgers for dinner. Grandma was in the
garden digging the soil for the Fall planting. The boys were
binkying around (that means they were jumping, running in
circles, twisting their bodies in mid-air and clicking their heels
together). Papa was down the road, helping his nephew dig a

new warren. When, all of a sudden, there was a loud knock at our own warren door.

Mama took off her apron and sniffed the door. Then she stood back with a low growl and trembled. "Hide bunnies. I smell fox!" The hard knocking came again, and a loud voice said, "Open up. It's the Fox Den Administration."

Mama raised her paws ready to box the foxes and protect her kittens. Then, very slowly, she opened the door.

Three foxes stood there looking very official and snoopy. The biggest one stepped forward and showed Mama his badge. "Hello Mam, I'm Sergeant Vulpine of the Fox Den Administration. We are looking for Penelope Rabbit." He took another step in, "Do you know where she is?"

Mama thumped the ground to warn him. "Please Sir, do not come into my warren. When I see Penelope Rabbit, I will tell her that you are looking for her." She tried to close the door, but just then Grandma Bunny hopped in from the back garden and asked, "What is going on here?"

The foxes smiled. "Are you Penelope Rabbit?" the sergeant asked.

"Yes, who wants to know?"

"We are from the Fox Den Administration, and we have a warrant for your arrest."

"What?" said Grandma Bunny. "What have I done wrong?"

"We have a report that you were treating Old Mr. Beaver with your herbal remedies."

"His foot was saved because of my herbal remedies."

"But you are not a doctor, Mrs. Rabbit, and herbal remedies are not considered safe medicine. You," the big fox sneered, as he reached out and handcuffed Grandma Bunny, "were practicing medicine without a doctor's license."

Grandma kicked with her back feet and shouted, "You can't do this." But they dragged her out the door and down the road.

We visit Grandma Bunny at the Fox Den Jail.

7
Jail

We were all sniffling with tears when Papa came home. Mama told him what had happened, and he was very angry. "That stupid, greedy Fox Den Administration. They receive so much money from the big drug and pharmaceutical companies. They just don't want any competition from Mother Nature. Mama, let's go see if we can get Grandma Bunny out of jail."

*****

The old, hollow-log jail, surrounded by foxes, was a frightening place. I would have hopped straight home as fast as I could without even trying to get in, but Papa was persistent, and they finally let us wait for Grandma Bunny. I trembled and thumped the ground the whole time.

Two fox guards led Grandma Bunny to the cage door. Her hind legs were shackled with rope. It made me very angry to see her this way. She hadn't done anything bad. I lifted my boxing paws, "Why are they treating you like this, Grandma?"

"I yelled at them," she answered. "I told them that the animals should know how to heal themselves...that they shouldn't have to run to doctors to fix every little thing. I told them that it is the animal's birthright to know what plants and foods in the forest will make them well. I told them that it is my responsibility and the responsibility of every creature, to teach the young ones all the wisdom we know. They didn't like what I had to say."

Then she looked us straight in the eyes and said, "If I never get out of this place, I want you to remember this: Don't let anyone take away your right to heal yourself and your family with the laws and plants of Nature." She held our gaze.

James took Grandma Bunny's paw, "Grandma, you are a great bunny."

With a nervous laugh Grandma asked, "Why is that, James?"

"Well, you haven't done anything bad, and still you have been put in jail. Mama says that those who are in power are afraid of great animals. So, you must be great."

Grandma sighed, "I don't know how great I am, but my heart is good, and my intentions are always to help, not harm. What the FDA is doing is wrong. They are being motivated by greed and not by what is right or by the goodness in their hearts." Then she looked at Papa and said, "You better get these bunnies home. They've had a long, frightening day. Oh, and anyone who comes to see me next, please bring some chamomile, catnip and fennel tea. My nerves and digestion are shot in this place."

*****

At home that night, we were all very sad. We held paws together and asked the Great Spirit of the Forest to bring Grandma Bunny back home again, and for the Fox Den Administration to leave her alone. Then we snuggled all together in the warren and tried to sleep.

The next day Mama packed a basket full of fresh grasses and a big thermos of chamomile, catnip and fennel tea for Grandma Bunny. She said, "Chamomile and catnip will help Grandma relax and the fennel will help her stomach." Bunnies always get upset stomachs when they are under stress.

*****

At the jail, when we handed Grandma Bunny a cup of tea, she took a big sniff and drank in the aroma.

"Ahhh, my friends, healing me even here." She was referring to the herbs. Herbs were much more to Grandma Bunny than just medicine or food. She spoke to them, and in an unusual way, they spoke to her.

I touched Grandma Bunny's paw, "Grandma. Papa has been telling everyone in the forest what the Fox Den Administration has done to you. I don't know what the animals are going to do, but they are going to do something."

Grandma smiled gratefully and wiped a tear from her eyes. "Thank you for standing by me."

Mama and I hugged her close. "We'll always stand by you," Mama said. "Rabbits are very strong, loyal and dependable."

8

Lies and Letters

The next day, an article appeared in the Forest Ought to Know Newspaper. It was an interview with Sargent Vulpine from the FDA. He stated that one foolish Penelope Rabbit had been recommending and administering herbal medicine to the forest animals, without a doctor's license. That was against the law. "We are not going to allow her to hop around the forest telling the animals fabrications about how to heal themselves. Animals should go to their doctors for solid advice."

The article made a lot of animals angry because they did not fully trust the FDA nor their doctors. Many doctors talked down to them in a snooty sort of way…as if they knew all the answers…as if the animals were stupid and didn't know what was wrong with them, or how to heal themselves without pharmaceutical drugs.

Many doctors had closed their minds to the natural healing plants of the forest and only gave the animals manufactured drugs. However, the manufactured drugs made the animals sick, sometimes sicker than they were to begin with. It is true that some doctors recommended natural herbs, but those doctors were shunned by the establishment - for not administering the "standard of care."

"No one knows everything," Grandma Bunny would say, "and even doctors are capable of mistakes and ignorance."

Grandma Bunny made every animal feel valuable. She trusted their instincts and valued their opinions. In turn, the animals trusted her. So, when Papa hopped through the forest with the news of what had happened to Grandma Bunny, almost all the animals were ready to do whatever they could to help her.

They met in the Gathering Glade, growled, talked and finally wrote a petition to the Fox Den Administration. (See the next page)

To the Fox Den Administration

We, the animals of this forest, request that you release Penelope Rabbit from jail, and that you allow her to take back her important place in our community.

It is true that she is not your kind of doctor, but she understands the laws of Nature. She is a Nature Doctor. She teaches us about the wild plants and the foods of the forest – which ones that can heal us, and those that can harm us. She teaches us how to keep ourselves well and how to heal ourselves instead of relying on the medical establishment for everything. She teaches us that doctors have a place in our forest, especially in emergencies and severe illnesses, but for chronic and minor illnesses, Mother Nature has the best answers.

She promotes that each one of us must take responsibility for our own health, that doctors and herbalists alike can offer advice, but that the final decisions should always lie with the animals themselves.

It has always been her hope that someday the doctors, the herbalists and the animals would work together and combine their wisdom. Then we would have "good medicine."

Penelope Rabbit is vital to our lives, and we request that you release her at once!

Sincerely,

The animals all signed the letter, and to show their vast support of Grandma Bunny. Then they walked in one huge procession, to deliver What they had written.

With all the animals descending upon them, the foxes became a bit nervous. Their livelihoods depended upon their well-paying jobs at the FDA.

Mr. Beaver lumbered forward and handed Sergeant Vulpine the petition letter.

Sargent Vulpine took a nervous breath and read the letter carefully. "I can see that Penelope Rabbit is very important to you all," he said. "But, you should know that her herbal remedies can be dangerous to your health."

Bear stood up on his hind legs and growled, "Let her go free. We know which plants are dangerous!"

Sargent Vulpine hesitated as all the animals pressed in on him. Finally, he opened the door and let Grandma Bunny out. "On the condition," he told her, holding her back, "that you promise not to recommend herbs for specific illnesses and definitely not administer them, because you are not a doctor. You may, however, continue teaching and growing certain herbs that the animals request."

The animals all nodded. This was acceptable to them. Grandma Bunny was released, and everyone was very happy to have made a difference. Bear and Mr. Beaver slapped a high five, and Dr. Bieler Mouse, who was an herbalist at heart, said he would stop by the warren with some of his Healing Soup for Grandma Bunny. My little bunny brothers ran around happily, twisting their bodies and clicking their heels together - what bunnies do when they are really happy.

Unfortunately, Grandma's fur was all matted and dirty from her ordeal. We took her home and gave her a cup of hot chamomile, catnip and fennel tea. Mama made root soup and seed bread, and Jerome and I licked her paws and fur to make her clean again. The frogs were so happy to have Grandma Bunny home that they sang a long, beautiful song for her. With all of this love, Grandma Bunny fell asleep, curled up, at home in our burrow. "Let her rest," Mama said. "Sleep is the best medicine. That is when the body heals itself."

The frogs are so happy that Grandma Bunny is home that
they sing a long, beautiful song to help her sleep.

The Wisdom of the Forest

The next morning when I woke up, Grandma Bunny was gone. Worried, I hopped around the burrow looking for her, but she was nowhere to be found. Finally, just letting my feet lead the way, I hopped to the meadow where I saw Grandma Bunny picking rose hips.

"It is past the first frost," she called out, "a little late, but I think the rose hips are still full of Vitamin C."

I hopped over and started picking rosehips with her.

Grandma Bunny stopped and looked up at the morning clouds, just parting to let the sun shine down on us.

"You know Jenny," she said. "I've been thinking. The Fox Den Administration is very unpredictable. We never know which rights they will try to take away next. If we want the wisdom of the Forest to continue, we need to share everything we know with the young animals. We do not want the next generation to forget. We need to encourage them to share the wisdom with their children…and their children…on and on, so that the wisdom becomes such an integral part of our culture that it cannot be erased by anyone. I'd like you to help me, Jenny. Together we can lead herb walks and classes for the young animals and anyone else who wants to come. With Ba's help (Ba lives on the farm near where we live), maybe we can even write a few books. Everyone who wants to, should know how to heal herself or himself."

I smiled really big, "I like that idea, Grandma, and I'd love to help you. Maybe, even DR Griffis will draw some pictures of us?"

"Good idea," she said, continuing to pick the rose hips, "We'll start tomorrow."

Grandma Bunny and me picking wild rosehips.

Grandma Bunny's

Recipe Section

Use Organic food and herbs whenever possible.

And remember,

healthy, organic food is your best medicine!

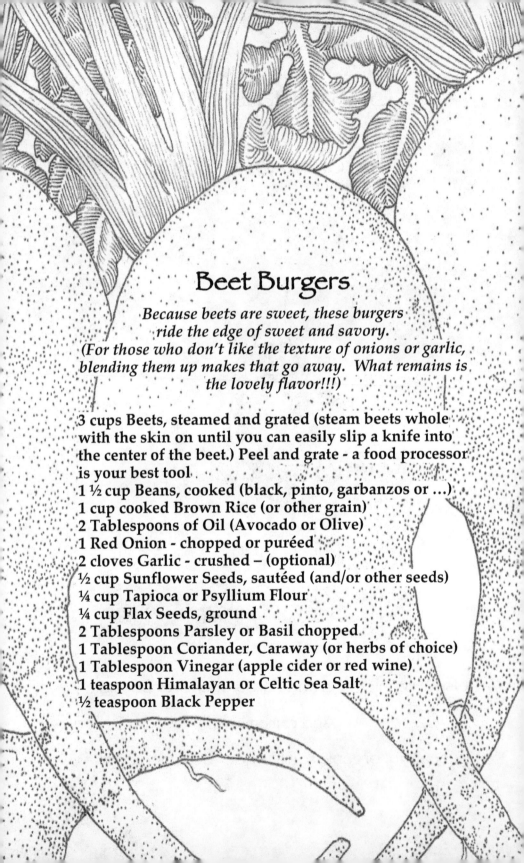

Beet Burgers

*Because beets are sweet, these burgers
ride the edge of sweet and savory.
(For those who don't like the texture of onions or garlic,
blending them up makes that go away. What remains is
the lovely flavor!!!)*

3 cups Beets, steamed and grated (steam beets whole
with the skin on until you can easily slip a knife into
the center of the beet.) Peel and grate - a food processor
is your best tool
1 ½ cup Beans, cooked (black, pinto, garbanzos or ...)
1 cup cooked Brown Rice (or other grain)
2 Tablespoons of Oil (Avocado or Olive)
1 Red Onion - chopped or puréed
2 cloves Garlic - crushed – (optional)
½ cup Sunflower Seeds, sautéed (and/or other seeds)
¼ cup Tapioca or Psyllium Flour
¼ cup Flax Seeds, ground
2 Tablespoons Parsley or Basil chopped
1 Tablespoon Coriander, Caraway (or herbs of choice)
1 Tablespoon Vinegar (apple cider or red wine)
1 teaspoon Himalayan or Celtic Sea Salt
½ teaspoon Black Pepper

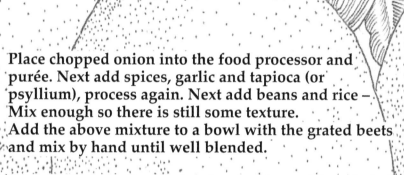

Place chopped onion into the food processor and purée. Next add spices, garlic and tapioca (or psyllium), process again. Next add beans and rice – Mix enough so there is still some texture.
Add the above mixture to a bowl with the grated beets and mix by hand until well blended.

*Use a wide mouth canning jar ring for making the burger shape.

Place canning jar lid on griddle, set at low/med heat. Ba likes a well- seasoned cast iron pan. Fill with mixture and cook until brown on one side then flip over and brown the other side. Let cool 5 min to solidify and to help it keep its shape. Serve on a bun with favorite condiments. Left overs can be cooled and frozen, with parchment paper between, to be saved for a quick meal later.

VARIATIONS:
Other vegetables can be substituted or mixed with the beets, such as carrots, zucchini, rutabaga, broccoli, kale, etc… use your imagination.
You can add Brewer's Yeast or ½ teaspoon Cayenne Pepper for a little kick.

Grandma Bunny's Nut Loaf

(Using What You Have)

2 cups Beans or Lentils of your choice (cooked)
2 cups Grains of your choice i.e.: Cooked brown rice or millet, rolled or quick oats, crushed whole grain cereal flakes or bread crumbs.
½ cup Nuts or Nut Butter of your choice (chopped or ground)
½-1 cup Liquid i.e.: broth from steamed or cooked vegetables, homemade nut or grain milk, tomato juice or tomato sauce …
Stick It Together: Choose one:
  3 Tablespoons tapioca, arrowroot or psyllium flour;
1/2 cup cooked   oatmeal
½-1 Tablespoon Herb Seasonings of your choice i.e.: cumin, coriander, sweet basil, Italian seasoning, oregano, parsley flakes, rosemary, sage, garlic or onion powder, nutritional yeast, Bragg's Liquid Amino's
1 Onion – chopped or pureed
2 cloves Garlic - crushed
Himalayan or Celtic Sea Salt and Pepper to taste

General Nut Loaf Directions: Mix all wet ingredients together, then the dry ones, then mix all together. Blend ½ in a food processor, then mix all together. Press into an oiled loaf pan and bake at 350 F for 45 minutes. Serve with a light gravy.

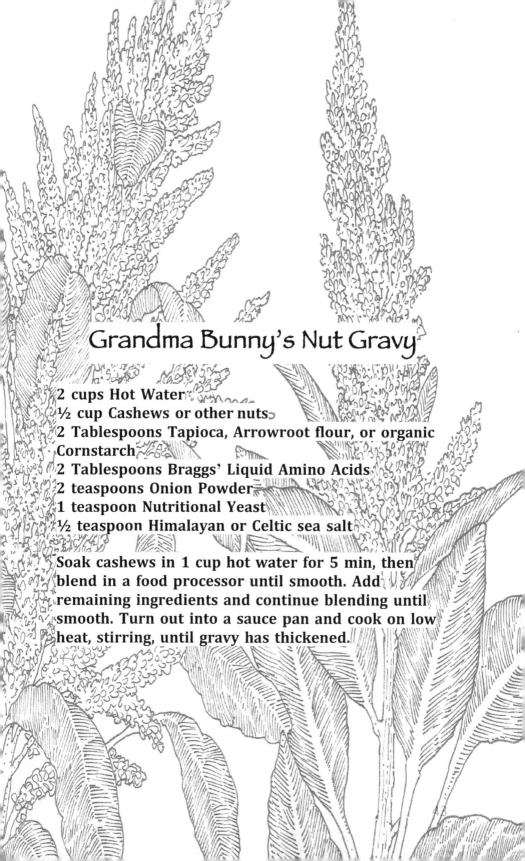

Grandma Bunny's Nut Gravy

2 cups Hot Water
½ cup Cashews or other nuts
2 Tablespoons Tapioca, Arrowroot flour, or organic Cornstarch
2 Tablespoons Braggs' Liquid Amino Acids
2 teaspoons Onion Powder
1 teaspoon Nutritional Yeast
½ teaspoon Himalayan or Celtic sea salt

Soak cashews in 1 cup hot water for 5 min, then blend in a food processor until smooth. Add remaining ingredients and continue blending until smooth. Turn out into a sauce pan and cook on low heat, stirring, until gravy has thickened.

Adventure Nut
Bread

1 cup sunflower seeds
½ cup flax seeds (ground)
1 cup rolled oats
2 Tablespoons chia seeds
2 Tablespoons psyllium seed husks
1 teaspoon Himalayan or Celtic sea salt
1 Tablespoon olive or melted coconut oil
1 ½ cup water or tea
3 large dates chopped
½ teaspoon cinnamon

Mix all ingredients in a bowl.
Press into a loaf pan and let sit overnight to absorb
the moisture.
Preheat oven to 350 F/175 C
Place loaf in the middle rack and bake for 1 hour,
until it sounds hollow when you tap it.
Let cool before slicing.
Store bread in a tightly sealed container for up to
five days. After slicing, you can freeze it and take
one slice at a time, as needed.

Healing Soup
From Doctor Bieler Mouse

Dr. Mouse suggests adding this healing soup to your daily diet whenever possible.

4 medium Zucchini squash, sliced
1-pound String Beans, ends removed and chopped
2 sticks Celery, chopped
1 bunch Parsley, chopped and stems removed
Fresh Herb Bouquet - Herbs such as: Parsley stems, Thyme, Rosemary, Tarragon or Savory, tied together with organic hemp or cotton string.
1-quart spring water or purified water.
1 teaspoon Sea Salt or Bragg's Liquid Aminos
1 tablespoon Olive Oil

Put zucchini, string beans, celery and herb bouquet into your soup pot with water and cook till bright green (ideally). Remove from heat and fish out the bouquet, then add chopped parsley leaves.
Purée soup with a blender (an immersion blender is easiest but not necessary).

Serve in a cup and season with Olive Oil and Himalayan or Celtic Sea Salt or Bragg's Liquid Aminos to taste. Some like a dollop of yogurt too!

Purslane Lasagna

Purslane is a gift from the Great Spirit of the Forest
It nourishes and protects the animals who eat it.
And remember, people are animals too

1 big bunch of Purslane, washed well and chopped
1 box of Lasagna Noodles – no boil noodles are easiest
1 quart Tomato-based Pasta Sauce
1 container (15 oz) Ricotta Cheese
16 oz Mozzarella Cheese (2 cups) - grated
3 cloves crushed Garlic
1 Bunch Fresh Basil – sliced
1 Tablespoon Italian Seasoning
1 teaspoon of Himalayan or Celtic Sea Salt
1 can Black Olives

Heat oven to 350 F.
Combine Ricotta Cheese, 1 cup of Mozzarella Cheese, Garlic,
Italian Seasoning, Basil and Salt. Mix well.
Oil baking dish and put a thin layer of pasta sauce on the
bottom.
Place one layer of Noodles – don't let them touch as they
will expand when they cook.
Cover Noodles with a thick layer of chopped Purslane.
Cover Purslane with the Cheese mixture
Spread ½ the Black Olives over the Cheese Mixture
Cover with Noodles.
Cover Noodles with remaining Pasta Sauce.
Top with the last cup of Mozzarella Cheese and Black Olives.
Cover with aluminum foil and bake for 50 minutes. Remove
foil and bake another 10 minutes. Let cool 15 minutes so
you don't burn yourself.

Purslane is very high in Omega 3 fatty acids. You can use purslane
wherever you would use spinach.

Spearmint Zest Hummus

3 cups cooked Garbanzo beans (or other beans of choice)
3 Tablespoons Sesame Tahini
3 cloves of crushed Garlic
6 Tablespoons Extra Virgin Olive Oil
3 Tables spoons Lemon Juice
¼ cup fresh Spearmint – chopped
½ teaspoon of Himalayan or Celtic Sea Salt
Zest (grated rind) of one or two lemons

Place Beans, Tahini, Garlic, Olive Oil, Lemon Juice and Salt
into a food processor and mix until you have the right,
smooth consistency. Add more bean water (liquor) if
necessary. Taste to see if it needs more lemon or salt. Add if
you think so.
Add Spearmint and process again.
PS: for a change, you can also use other green herbs, like
fresh basil, arugula, mizuna, rosemary. Heck, why not
roses...

Serve in a beautiful bowl topped with extra chopped
Spearmint, additional Lemon Zest and chopped Pistachios or
other nuts. Set out with raw vegetables or crackers.

Calming Tea

1 cup Chamomile Flowers
1/4 cup Catnip Leaves
¼ cup Fennel Seeds, crushed

Blend dry herbs together and store in a sealed jar.
Put 1 teaspoon of the mixture per cup into a tea infuser and
pour hot water over the top. Let sit for at least 5 minutes.
Sweeten if you want with honey or sweetener of your
choice, and, if you want, some nut mylk of your choice.

Happy Tummy Tea

1/2 cup Peppermint leaves
1 cup Spearmint leaves
1/4 cup Catnip leaves

Crush and mix herbs together in a bowl, then store in a well-sealed jar. Use @ 3 tablespoon of herbs to make a pot of tea. Let steep for 5 min. Strain. Sweeten if you want, with a teaspoon of real honey or sweetener of your choice. Top off with milk of your choice.

49

Sunflower Seed Cookies

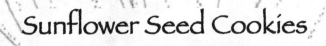

1/2 cup almond flour
1 cup sunflower flour
3 Tablespoons arrowroot or tapioca flour
Zest of 1 grated Meyer Lemon
(or Orange or Mandarin Zest)
1/2 teaspoon Baking Powder
1/2 teaspoon Almond Extract
1/3 cup Maple Syrup
1/4 cup Ghee or Coconut Oil, melted
3 Tablespoons Dried Fruit of your choice
1/4 teaspoon of Himalayan or Celtic Sea Salt

PREPARATION:
Preheat oven to 350 F. Line a baking sheet with parchment
paper.
In two bowls, mix one with dry ingredients, one with wet
ingredients. When well combined, add the wet ingredients
to the dry ones and mix together.
Use a teaspoon or cookie scoop and drop onto parchment
paper 2 inches apart.
Bake for 15 minutes until golden around the edges. Remove
cookies from oven and allow to cool before taking them off
the cookie sheet.

Almond Cookie Cut-Outs

¾ cup Almond meal
1/3 cup Tapioca or Arrowroot flour
1 Tablespoon Coconut Flour
½ teaspoon Baking Soda
¼ teaspoon of Himalayan or Celtic Sea Salt
¼ cup Coconut Oil, melted
¼ cup Maple Syrup
1 teaspoon real Almond Flavoring
Or 2 teaspoons real Vanilla Flavoring

Mix dry ingredients thoroughly, then the wet ones, then mix
them all together.
Place dough between two pieces of parchment paper and
roll out dough to ¼ inch thick. Place rolled out dough in the
fridge for 30 minutes.
Preheat the oven to 350 F.
Line cookie sheet with parchment paper.
Cut out shapes with cookie cutter and place on parchment.
Bake for 10-12 minutes until golden around the edges. Let
cool before removing from cookie sheet. Roll the scraps
back into a ball and roll it out again, replace in the
refrigerator, then use cookie cutters again. Decorate, if you
want to...

Interesting Rabbit Facts

In this book, I am using the European Rabbit as my model. This is simply because they are more like humans, born with their eyes closed and dependent on their mothers. Most wild rabbits are born with their eyes open and are only nursed 2-3 times before they are left to their own devices.

Super happy rabbits practice a cute behavior known as a "binky" or "boinking." They jump up in the air and twist and spin around and click their back feet together! A baby rabbit is called a kit, a female is called a doe, and a male is a buck. A group of rabbits is called a herd. Rabbits are herbivores, eating a diet entirely of grasses and other plants.

European rabbits have lots of babies and can have multiple litters each year, giving birth to up to 9 babies, known as "kittens." In the wild they're born helpless in a shallow hole lined with grass and their mama's fur. Mother rabbits in the wild spend only a few moments each day with their babies in order to avoid drawing attention to them from predators. The babies grow quickly and continue to live together as a family.

Rabbits are crepuscular, meaning that they are awake at night and sleep during the day. Rabbits purr when they are content. It sounds like teeth chattering quietly or lightly chomping.

Rabbits eat their poop. Yes, that is right, for a second round of digestion. Their night droppings are called "cencotropes." The round poops are what is left after the 2nd round of digestion.

Rabbits Are Not Good First Pets for Children.

While rabbits are endearing, they require a lot of effort – more than just feeding. They need a mostly grass diet and wood to chew on, otherwise their teeth and nails get too long. They need a large, safe environment to roam (free of electrical wires and other animals that may terrorize them), dirt to dig, places to hide, toys to play with, specialized grooming of nails and hair, and gentle, quiet affection.

While they are most happy with a second rabbit for company, their territorial natures can make them very dangerous, even deadly to other rabbits, and much care must be given to introduce one to another. Also, rabbits need a special veterinarian who understands the particulars of rabbits.

Please read about how to care for your pet bunny before you get one! As Grandma Bunny says, "Learn all you can, and be wise.

Jenifer Victoria Bliss (Ba), born in Santa Cruz and raised in Paradise, California, is a mother, grandmother, writer, researcher, artist and Early Childhood Educator. She studied with herbalist Kathi Keville in the early 1990s and co-developed a medicinal herb nursery, High Sierra Herbs. She has worked with children and families as a Home Visitor, Preschool Teacher, Caregiver and Supervisor. She studied with Claire Braz-Valentine, mentor, writer and poet in Butte County. Jenifer is a founding member of the Sierra Muses Writer's Workshop. She currently lives on an organic farm in the Sierra Nevada Mountains, with her husband Amigo Bob, where she does research and field studies for the Felix Gillet Institute. Her passion is spending time in Nature and encouraging children to develop relationships with the natural world. She developed Faerie Camp, an experiential camp for young children: *www.faeriecamps.com*. In addition, she has published **The Young Centaur, Book 1, The Life of Kheiron, Wise Centaur of Ancient Greece**, available at Amazon. Other books are in the works…

David Randolph Griffis was born in Texas and raised in Missouri in a small college town. He is self-taught, his education being off the shelf of the libraries and bookstores where, as he says, "Centuries of accumulated skills and techniques, with the story to back, are at your fingertips in all the oldest of modern mediums: books." He designed the chandelier artwork as part of the Georgia State Capital Restoration Project. He is a beloved father and grandfather and has published two coloring books of his original art, featuring a portion of his portfolio of vegetable and flower illustrations: **A Coloring Book for Discerning Colorists, Vol. 1 and Vol. 2**, available on Amazon. David lives off the grid in his studio and home where he is continually inspired to interpret the natural world into drawings, paintings, woodcarvings and ceramics.

Enjoy the flowers as you hop through life.

CPSIA information can be obtained
at www.ICGtesting.com
Printed in the USA
LVHW011607131220
674080LV00031B/882

9 780991 210244